April 1978

Best wishes —

Susan Jeschke

THE DEVIL DID IT

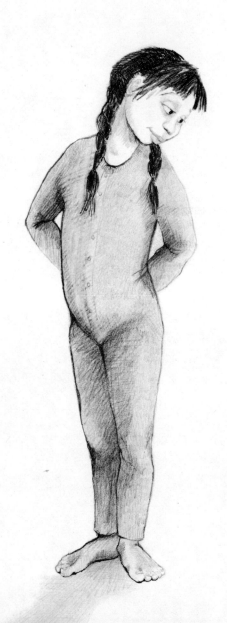

THE DEVIL DID IT

Susan Jeschke

Holt, Rinehart and Winston
New York

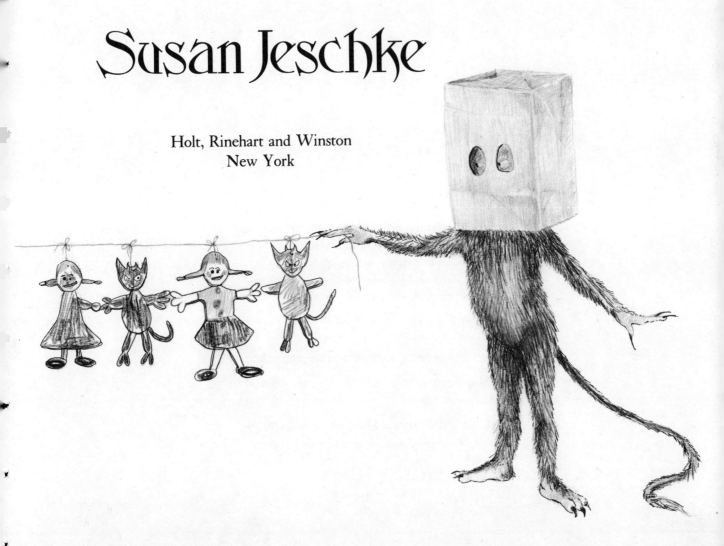

For Orfea Barricelli

Library of Congress Cataloging in Publication Data

Jeschke, Susan.
   The Devil did it.

   SUMMARY: Always blamed for her devil's
pranks, Nana determines to outwit him and treat
him well.
   [1. Devil's—Fiction] I. Title.
PZ7.J553De   [E]   75–6549
ISBN 0–03–014506–6

Mama separated Nana's hair into two parts and began to comb it.

"Ow!" Nana said.

"Sorry. It's full of knots," Mama said.

"How did the knots get there?"

"How? The devil did it, that's how. Now hold still," said Mama.

Mama finished combing Nana's hair and sent her out to play.

All day long Nana thought about the devil.

That night, Nana lay in bed listening for devil noises. At first she heard only the ticking of the clock. Then she heard another sound, a scratching from under the bed.

"It's the devil," Nana thought. "Ma! Ma!" she cried.

The door opened and Mama and Papa appeared.

"The devil is under my bed," Nana said.

"What nonsense," said Mama, bending to look.

"Absolutely nothing," Papa said.

Papa brought Nana a glass of milk and some cookies. Then Mama told her to go to sleep.

Again alone, Nana listened to the tick-tock of the clock. Then, again came the *scratch-scratching* from under the bed. Nana hid herself under the blanket. Next she heard a new noise. *Slurp-slurp, cr-runch,* then a voice saying, "Ummmmm." Carefully, Nana peeked out from under her blanket. And there, looking back at her, was a furry creature with large eyes, pointed ears, and—horns.

"The devil!" Nana cried.

She jumped out of bed and ran out into the hall, where she collided with Grandma.

"Grandma! Grandma!" Nana cried, throwing her arms around her grandmother, "there's a devil in my room."

"There is?" Grandma said. She went to the broom closet, took out a broom, and led the way to Nana's room.

"Agh. I can't see him," Grandma said, poking around under the bed with the broom.

"Oh, look," Nana said. "The devil ate my cookies and milk."

"A hungry demon," Grandma said. She took Nana by the hand. "Come and sleep with me," she said.

Grandma fell asleep at once but Nana couldn't sleep. She climbed out of the bed and went back to her room. And there, sleeping on her pillow, was the devil.

"Get out!" Nana cried.
The devil awoke and laughed at her.
Nana threw a pillow at him.

The devil grabbed the blanket. Nana grabbed her wooden sword. "Shoo!" she yelled.

CRASH! Down came the lamp. The devil laughed again and ran out. Nana ran after him.

"I know where you're hiding," she said.
The devil aimed the nozzle at her.
"Yeow . . . you little monster," she yelled.
RRRRIP . . . went the curtain.

Suddenly Papa was standing in the doorway.

"The devil did it, Papa," Nana said.

"What devil? I don't see any devil," Papa said. "If you don't go to sleep right now I'll give you something that can be seen."

Nana picked up her sword and hurried past Papa.

The devil jumped into bed ahead of her, plumped up the pillow, and went to sleep. Nana was too tired to object. She, too, soon fell asleep.

The next morning Nana told Grandma all that had happened.
"These demons," Grandma sighed. "They come and go. He'll go.
You'll see. But treat him well while he's here."
This was very hard for Nana to do because the devil delighted in
making trouble. And she was always blamed for his pranks.

The day her cousin Joey stayed over, all of his clothes disappeared.
When they reappeared on the dog, Pepper, Nana was blamed.
"I didn't do it. The devil did it," she said.

"The devil did it," Nana said when Papa's socks were found in the refrigerator.

"It must have been the devil," Nana said when Mama asked about the turkey hanging from the chandelier.

"A devil named Nana?" Mama said.

Only Grandma seemed to believe Nana. She gave Nana an oddly shaped bottle and told her it was a devil-catcher. If the devil didn't leave on his own, Grandma said, the bottle would catch him.

But that is not what happened. The devil liked the bottle. He snatched it away from Nana and kept it for himself.

Little by little Nana got used to her devil.

She learned to ignore him.

To play with him.

Even to out-devil him. And that she enjoyed the most.

One day she grabbed him, tied him up, and combed his fur.
"We're just alike," she said.
The devil huffed at her. She let him go.

All that day the devil sulked. Nana put her favorite rubber snake in a basket and gave it to him.

"A present for you," she said. He pushed the present away and hid under the bed.

"What's the matter?" Nana said.

The devil only growled in reply. Nana shrugged and went off to play by herself.

That night, Nana brought a dish of cookies to her room. She was happy to find the devil there and offered him some cookies. As the devil helped himself to the cookies, a tear rolled down his cheek.

Then he picked up his basket. He put the cookies in first, then the snake. But the devil-catcher would not fit.

"Phooey on this!" the devil said, flinging it aside.

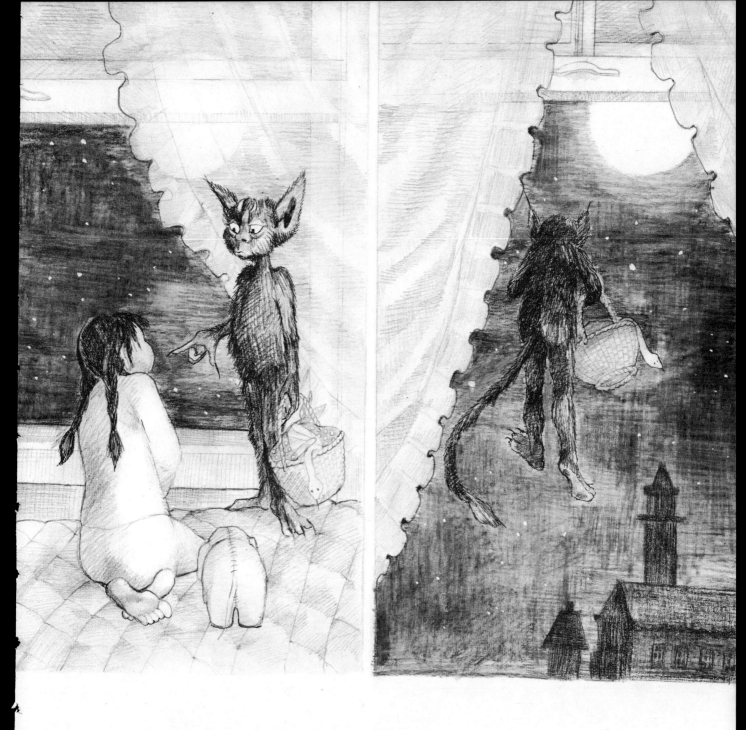

"What are you doing?" Nana asked.

"I'm leaving," he said.

"But why? I like you," Nana said.

"That's why!" the devil said. "You aren't afraid of me anymore. I can't do anything to annoy you or make you unhappy. You don't respect me. You even like me. SO . . . Goodby!" He turned abruptly and walked out the window, disappearing into the night.

Nana stood at the window for a long time.

The devil-catcher gleamed and winked at her in the moonlight.

Nana took it and went to Grandma's room.

"I don't need this. My devil's gone," she said, beginning to cry.

Grandma took Nana on her lap and began to rock her. "These demons, that's how they are. They come and go, come and go. . . ."

"Do you think he'll come back?" Nana asked sleepily.

But before Grandma could answer, Nana was fast asleep.

ABOUT THE AUTHOR

Susan Jeschke was born in Cleveland, Ohio, and presently lives in Brooklyn, New York.

Ms. Jeschke attended classes at the School of Visual Arts, and the Brooklyn Museum School, studying printmaking, sculpture, and illustration.

She is the author/illustrator of FIREROSE, selected as one of the (ALA) Notable Books of the Year, 1974, and of SIDNEY.

ABOUT *Firerose*

*"One of the freshest, most imaginative books to appear lately." *The Booklist*
"A lovingly illustrated story." *Saturday Review*
*"A wonderfully down-to-earth fantasy." *School Library Journal*

ABOUT *Sidney*

*Starred review in *School Library Journal*.
"A truly droll and offbeat series of adventures in a book which will add to the growing list of Ms. Jeschke's admirers." *Publisher's Weekly*

ABOUT THE BOOK

The text is set in Janson and the display type in Skjald. The pictures are grease pencil and ink drawings.